See me, HEAR ME, know Me

by Denise Lewis Patrick

American Girl®

ABOUT THE AUTHOR

Denise Lewis Patrick grew up in Natchitoches, Louisiana. Lots of relatives lived nearby, so there was always someone watching out for her and always someone to play with. Every week, Denise and her brother went to the library, where she would read and dream in the children's room overlooking a wonderful river. She wrote and illustrated her first book when she was ten—she glued yellow cloth to cardboard for the cover and sewed the pages together on her mom's sewing machine. Today, Denise lives in New Jersey, where she still loves to read, write, and make books.

ABOUT THE ILLUSTRATOR

Courtney Lovett was born and raised in Maryland, surrounded by a loving and supportive community. As soon as she could pick up a pencil, she loved to draw the cartoons she saw on TV. Courtney drew every day and carried a sketchbook with her wherever she went. She earned a fine arts degree in illustration and animation so she could create stories that spark a passion for art in other kids. Today, she still lives in her hometown, where she illustrates books and teaches at a local art studio.

ADVISERS FOR MAKENA'S STORY

M. Lucero Ortiz is a human rights attorney with a focus on family and immigration law. Prior to joining Kids in Need of Defense as the Deputy Director for KIND Mexico, she represented migrant families and unaccompanied children before the Departments of Homeland Security and Justice.

Deborah Rivas-Drake is a professor of psychology and education at the University of Michigan, where she studies how teens navigate issues of race, ethnicity, racism, and xenophobia. She wrote the award-winning book *Below the Surface: Talking with Teens about Race, Ethnicity, and Identity*.

Deanna Singh leads workshops on creating impactful social and personal change. She founded Flying Elephant, a consulting firm to help women and people of color become social entrepreneurs. She has written four children's books about racism, including *A Smart Girl's Guide: Race & Inclusion*.

Naomi Wadler is a 14-year-old activist concerned with racial justice. She focuses on optimism in the face of current events. She's interested in how journalism and media can influence others and make the world a better place. At age 11 she was the youngest speaker at the 2018 March for Our Lives rally in Washington, DC.

Yasmine Mabene is a student at Stanford University. A teen activist, she is the California State Director of March for Our Lives, a youth organization working to prevent gun violence, and the social media coordinator of Earth Uprising, an international youth-led organization that works to fight climate change through education.

Hi! We're Makena, Evette, and Maritza. We want to live in a world where everyone is treated fairly and with respect. We believe that if we work together, we can build a future that works for all of us. Best of all, we don't need to wait until we grow up to make a difference—we can do it right now! Together, we have the power to create the kind of world we want: *a world by us*.

MAKENA WILLIAMS

Makenashine

Aspire Academy besties Adeline and Najee

Hi! I'm Makena (pronounced ma-KAY-na) which means "happy one" in Swahili. I love art, cooking, and riding my bike, but my passion is fashion. My favorite colors are purple and glitter. I am 13 years old and go to Aspire Academy Middle School in Washington, DC. I live in Anacostia with my mom (Chandra), dad (Tony), and sister Amari (she's 11).

My newest friends, Maritza and Evette

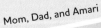
Mom, Dad, and Amari

BACK IN STYLE
Chapter 1

"Makena! Wait!" My sister called after me, but I was way ahead of her. It wasn't until I pushed open the door of Cherry Blossoms that I stopped. I hadn't been inside my favorite clothing store for nearly a year, and I couldn't wait another second. During the pandemic, we had to do everything—school, work, shopping, even visiting family—at home and online. It had been hard not going anywhere and not seeing anyone, and now I was eager to be out in public again.

"Slow down!" Amari said when she caught up with me.

"No way," I teased. "This is the first time I get to pick out new clothes for school." In a few days I would be starting seventh grade, and unlike grade school, I wouldn't have to wear a uniform. I didn't have to wear a uniform last year either, but since school was remote, there hadn't been any back-to-school shopping. Today was a day for fashion, and I couldn't wait to see what I would find.

"Where should we start?" Aunt Belinda asked, coming into the store with Mom.

"Over here, Auntie Bling!" I said, heading toward the back. We went in one direction while Amari and Mom went another. As we wandered the store, I ran my hands along the racks, feeling the different fabrics against my skin. "Auntie Bling, check this out!" I pulled a cherry red sweater off a shelf. A pattern of tiny gold threads ran through it so that when you turned it a certain way, there was a little flash of light. I spotted a short orange plaid skirt and held both items up. "How's this?"

Auntie Bling studied the combination. "Wow, I see it!" she said, nodding. "I would never have put this mix together, but it works. It's so *you*, Makena."

I grinned. Auntie Bling is a stylist in Los Angeles, so that meant a lot to me. "The colors remind me of the kente cloth dress you brought me from your trip to Ghana," I said, putting the sweater and skirt back.

"I gave you that when you were four!" Auntie Bling said, sifting through the rack.

"Well, that dress was totally different from any of my other clothes," I said. "And when you told me each kente pattern has a special meaning, it blew my mind." I picked out a turquoise shirt decorated with butterflies and showed it to Auntie Bling.

Auntie Bling looked at the shirt and then handed me a skirt that faded from dark purple to light lavender. "Is that why you wore the kente dress to preschool every day?" she teased.

I nodded. "I even slept in it, dreaming that one day I might visit Ghana, too. It made me feel special. Like I had something no one else had."

"You still do," Auntie Bling insisted. "You have your own style, girl. Keep showing off your shine in those Instagram posts. I love seeing what you wear every day."

When school went virtual, I decided that I would *not* wear sweats all the time. Every night I picked out an outfit, and every morning I gave myself time to style it based on how I was feeling. Since I only showed up in one little square on a screen, I started taking selfies of my whole outfit and posting them online. A couple of my friends told me they looked forward to seeing what I wore. They said it made them feel normal at a time when things weren't. Pretty soon people started posting their outfits, too. I posted all summer, and I guess I'll keep doing it, even when we're back to school in person.

Back in person, I thought happily as I sifted through the store's racks. I can't wait to be with people again. I've missed that so much, and I've decided I'm not going to waste a single minute being shy. I'm going to make as many new friends as I can.

I had an armful of items when Auntie Bling and I caught up to Mom and Amari. "Makena, you're so lucky!" Amari said, admiring my choices.

"You're still getting some new things," Mom reminded her. "You're growing so fast these days."

"Look at that," I said, pointing to a top on a nearby mannequin. It had a border of fancy stitching around the neckline, and I wanted to take a picture of it.

"Amari, could you hold my stuff?" I asked, digging my phone out of my pocket.

"Chandra!" Auntie Bling called to Mom as I clicked a photo. "That looks like a dashiki!"

I lowered my phone. "Da-what?"

"A dashiki! It's a type of shirt based on traditional African clothing," Mom said. "Lots of Black men and women wore dashikis in the 1960s and 1970s to show their pride in our African heritage." Mom was using her librarian voice, but her face had that back-in-the-day look that she got when she talked about something from growing up.

Auntie Bling leaned toward me and Amari. "Your mom actually *made* her own dashiki!"

4

We stared at Mom, wide-eyed. As long as I could remember, it was Dad who helped us with crafts and school projects. Mom wasn't much of a maker.

"Mom, you *sewed* something?" Amari asked.

"Yes, I did!" she said proudly. "It was for a seventh-grade talent show. I recited a poem written by Nikki Giovanni. She is an outspoken Black poet, and I wanted to dress like her for the show, so I chose a dashiki."

"It was amazing," Auntie Bling said. "*She* was amazing!"

"It was scary," Mom said.

"Which part?" I asked. "The sewing, or being onstage in front of everybody?"

"Both!" Mom said without hesitation. "But I was proud of being a young Black woman, and the words I was reciting were important. So, I found my courage."

"That was really brave, Mom," I said.

Mom smiled. "When you feel strongly enough about something, you find a way to take action."

There were a lot of people waiting to check out, so Amari and I got in line while Mom and Auntie Bling kept shopping.

I was looking at my phone when Amari nudged me. She

motioned in front of us, where two White girls had stepped. I thought they were taking a shortcut to get to the other side of the store, but they just stood there.

"Excuse me," I said, "but this is a line."

Both of them were chewing gum, and one smacked it as she turned her head toward me. She looked like she was my age.

"This is a line?" she asked as though she didn't understand the concept.

Amari leaned around me. "Uh...yeah!"

"And the end of it"—I pointed over my shoulder—"is back there."

"But we were here before—" she said, raising her voice a little. A couple of people looked around. I wanted to raise my voice, too, but I didn't want to make a scene.

"No, you weren't!" A woman behind us frowned at them. "We're all waiting our turn, and you can, too."

"Oh. We didn't know," the other girl mumbled. She pulled her friend away. Amari and I watched them scurry to the very end of the line, six or seven people back.

"Couldn't she see—?" Amari asked.

"She saw what she wanted to see," I said. "And she didn't want to see us in line ahead of her." I took a step forward and pulled Amari with me. "Come on," I said. "The line is moving. Move on up."

TOGETHER AGAIN
Chapter 2

When we got home, Dad and Uncle Alex were in the kitchen. Uncle Alex was in full chef mode with multiple pots bubbling on the stove. He had his earbuds in and a black bandanna tied around his forehead. Dad was chopping vegetables.

"I'm glad you're back!" Dad said. "Top Chef over there needs somebody else to boss around!"

Dad wasn't entirely joking. My grandparents had owned Cook's Kitchen, a restaurant in Anacostia, our Washington, DC, neighborhood, for over forty years. Uncle Alex had been the head chef there for as long as I could remember. He'd taken over the business a few years ago when Gran and Grandad retired.

"I'll set the table," Mom said. She was the one member of the Cook family who didn't like to cook. Auntie Bling tried to lift the lid of one of the pans on the stove, but Uncle Alex slapped her hand away.

Amari and I dropped our shopping bags and washed our hands. "What can we do?" we asked Uncle Alex in unison.

He pulled out his earbuds. "The dishwashers have arrived!" he joked, gesturing to the sink full of dirty dishes.

"No way!" Amari cried.

"We want to help," I insisted.

Uncle Alex grinned. "Do you want to make chicken wings?" Chicken wings were one of Grandad's specialties. They were so popular at the restaurant that Uncle Alex had promised to never change any part of Grandad's secret recipe.

Everyone burst into a singsong chant.

> *Rudy's wings are the best,*
> *Oni-yum, garlic, lemon zest*
> *Red pepper, white pepper,*
> *Hot, hot, hot!*
> *Sizz, sizz, sizzle in the pot!*

Amari added some moves, so we all kept singing while she danced. Auntie Bling tried to copy what Amari was doing, which made Amari double over with laughter.

Suddenly, the kitchen lights flashed on and off and we all stopped singing. Then Auntie Bling let out a happy scream and ran to the front door. Gran and Grandad stood there, Grandad's hand on the light switch. "You all still singing that goofy song?" he teased as Auntie Bling wrapped him and Gran into a huge hug. "You were making so much noise that nobody heard the doorbell."

Amari and I raced over to pile into the hug. Mom and Dad followed. "The Cook Crew is together again!" Dad said.

Gran and Grandad had moved to North Carolina just before the pandemic started. They had been back to DC a couple of times in the last few months to see us and Uncle Alex, but this was the first time Auntie Bling had visited from California in over a year. We'd all called and messaged each other, of course, and our whole family did a weekly video call, but it wasn't the same as being together, in the same room, smooshed in the same hug.

"I hope nothing's burning," Grandad said, which sent the grown-ups back to the kitchen.

Gran put one arm around Amari and one around me. "I've been loving the snazzy outfits you put up online, Kay."

"Thanks," I grinned. "You should post *your* outfit," I said, admiring the intricate embroidery on her jacket. "You made that, didn't you?"

Gran nodded. "I enjoy having so much more time for needlework. I'll teach you if you want." She gave Amari a squeeze. "And thank *you* for sending us that clip of your basketball game!"

"You were flying down that court," Grandad said, making Amari blush. "Now, let's go see what's cooking!"

In the kitchen, Grandad lifted the lid on one of the pots and nodded. I could tell he was pleased that Uncle Alex had

made seafood and rice from the old menu. "Smelling good, son!" he said.

"It's one of the best sellers at the food truck," Uncle Alex said. He'd done his best to keep Cook's Kitchen going during the pandemic, but like so many small businesses, it didn't survive. Uncle Alex had to close the restaurant. A few months ago, he'd started a food truck called Cruisin' Cook.

"And now even more people get to try the best food in DC," I said, taking a basket of warm corn muffins to the dining room. "Uncle Alex is going to be at the food truck festival at the new community center next weekend!"

"That's great news," Gran said.

Grandad nodded. "Food brings people together."

"Well, this food's ready," Uncle Alex said. "Let's eat!"

After dinner, Gran wanted to see the new clothes we'd gotten on our shopping trip, so all us girls headed upstairs. Amari and I took turns showing her what we'd picked out, piling everything on the bed in Mom and Dad's room.

"Do you know what you're going to wear on your first day of school?" Gran asked.

"I do," Amari sighed. "Polo shirt and khaki pants. Boring."

"I'm not sure *what* to choose," I admitted.

"Well," Mom said, "how do you want others to see you?"

I thought about that for a moment. "I want everyone to know that I'm glad to be back at school and I want to make friends and I really like art and I—"

Amari laughed. "How can your clothes show all that?"

"Clothes make a statement," Auntie Bling explained. "Like that dashiki your mom made."

I'd never quite thought about my clothes that way before. As I sorted through the new items on the bed, I wondered what kind of statement I wanted to make. I was going to have fun figuring it out!

"I'm sorry I won't be here for your first day of school," Auntie Bling said. She was heading back to LA tomorrow.

"I am, too," Gran added. She and Grandad were going on their first cruise, and they were flying out on Monday.

"Well, you're all here now," Mom said, hugging Gran and Auntie Bling close.

I grinned. "And you can check out my page on Tuesday to see my middle school debut outfit!"

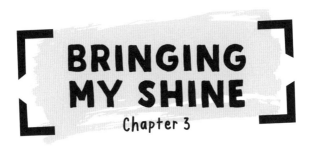

BRINGING MY SHINE

Chapter 3

Three days later, I stood in front of the mirror studying my outfit. I'd chosen the purple skirt that Auntie Bling had picked out at Cherry Blossoms. She said the style was called *ombre*, which means "shaded." I loved how the skirt shows off different versions of my favorite color. I added a black T-shirt with a swirl of purple. As I looked at the outfit now, I realized it still needed . . . something. I closed my eyes and focused on how I was feeling. I was nervous, but excited, too, like something I had been waiting for was finally about to begin. I opened my eyes and sifted through the basket of hair accessories on my dresser. I added three gold butterfly hair clips to my twists. Butterflies are a symbol of transformation, and I knew today would be full of big changes. When I tilted my head, the butterflies looked like they were taking off.

I picked up my phone, took a selfie, and posted my OOTD (outfit of the day) with the words, *"Transforming into a 7th grader! #OOTD #firstday #seventhgrade #backtoschool."*

I grabbed an extra hair clip, checked that I had my class schedule and house key, and headed downstairs. My whole family was waiting for me on the front porch.

"I know you'll have a great day!" Mom said, as she took my picture. "Do you have your key?"

"Yep," I said, patting my backpack.

Dad gave me a hug. "Be safe. Remember your sister."

"See you this afternoon," Amari said with a hint of sadness in her voice. It was the first time we wouldn't be walking to school together.

"Wear this today." I handed her a butterfly clip, and her face brightened.

"Really? Thanks, Makena!"

I skipped down the steps feeling like I could fly. Our neighbors Jerome and Stella were having coffee on their front stoop, and they waved when I went by. Jerome was Black and Stella was White, and they were both artists. They had a studio in their house, complete with a kiln. Stella had just started giving me pottery lessons. "Show that middle school what you can do!" Jerome called.

At the corner, Mr. Scott, the crossing guard, held up his sign for me to cross the street. I shook my head and turned left. "Okay, Makena! Moving on up!" he said.

As I headed for the train station, my phone buzzed. One, two, three texts. I kept walking and opened the first message.

Happy first day of school! Thinking about your statement.

It's 5 am in CA but I'm awake and seeing your outfit. You're shining, girl!

Do your thing, Kay! Don't walk and scroll . . .

Busted!

Two blocks later I reached the Metro entrance, swiped my pass, and went down the escalator. I walked along the platform and stopped near a neatly dressed woman. The tote bag she was carrying had a beautiful pattern that I couldn't stop staring at.

"Hey, Makena?" a familiar voice called over my shoulder. I turned around.

"Najee!" I blurted out to the boy walking toward me. He was taller than I remembered, and his usually bushy afro was trimmed into a close-cropped fade. "You're back!" I said, as the train pulled in. We hopped on together.

Najee and I had lived a few blocks away from each other since kindergarten, and we'd gone to elementary school together. Well, we had until school went remote, and everybody's lives went sideways. I knew his mom had gotten laid off. I hadn't seen him in over a year.

"Yeah. Mom got COVID. My sister and me spent some time with family in Brooklyn."

"Oh!" I swallowed hard. I tried to think of the right thing to say. "Is...um...how's she doing?"

"It was rough, you know?" Najee said, pushing his glasses up on his nose. "That virus was no joke. But Mom is okay now. Back working."

"I'm glad," I said, and I meant it. "So, are you going to school out-of-bounds, too?" I asked. That's what we call it when kids go to a public school outside their neighborhood.

"Yeah. Aspire Academy."

I couldn't believe it. "Me, too!"

Najee's face brightened. "Now I know someone in the building." He ducked his head to look out the window. "Our stop is next!"

We pushed our way to the doors as they opened. I stumbled out first. Najee barely made it out behind me before the doors closed on his shiny neon orange sneakers.

"Nice kicks!" I said.

He grinned. "And I see you still show off your style!"

We only had to walk two blocks before I caught sight of the school. A bright red and yellow banner flapping over the open doors read "Aspire to Success."

I stood still for a second, watching kids flow into the building. Aspire was much more diverse in both people and style. Instead of mostly Black kids, like at my old school, the students here were Latinx, Black, White, and mixed-race, too.

I stopped to search in my bag for my building map.

"Wow," Najee murmured. "All these faces—can you even see one that you recognize from virtual classes?"

When I looked up to answer, Najee was already sprinting over to some kids in DC United team jerseys.

"I don't, but I guess *you* do!" I smiled and headed inside.

The halls were crowded, and everyone seemed to know where they were going. I stepped to one side, unfolded my schedule, and double-checked my homeroom number.

A girl behind me said, "Oh! You've got two of the same teachers I have." She was leaning over my shoulder, looking at my schedule. Her hair was arranged in neat rows of beautifully twisted Bantu knots, and she had on multiple bracelets that clinked softly.

"Which classes?" I asked.

"Homeroom and algebra." She nodded at my hair clips. "Nice butterflies!"

"Thanks. I really like your bracelets," I said, pointing to her wrists. "I'm Makena."

"I know," she said. "I follow your posts."

"You do?" I asked. I must have looked surprised because the girl laughed. "Sorry," I said. "I just didn't think I'd run into any, um, followers."

"I'm Adeline," the girl said. She shook her arms to make the bracelets jingle as if they were instruments. "Can I walk with you to class?"

Now I laughed. "If you want, but I'm not sure where I'm going."

"We'll find it together," Adeline said. As we navigated the halls, we passed a boy wearing a T-shirt printed with a panther wrapped around him from front to back. An older girl rushed by with a knee-length, floaty jacket that looked as if it was covered with autumn leaves. *Their clothes are making statements!* I thought.

"It's strange to be in school and not see everyone in the same uniform," I said to Adeline.

She laughed. "Strange but fun."

In homeroom, Adeline and I sat next to each other. A tall woman with straight black hair introduced herself as Ms. Jacobs-Lee.

"Welcome to homeroom and social studies," Ms. Jacobs-Lee said cheerfully. She gave everyone a marker and pointed at the walls, which were hung with giant blank outlines of all seven continents. "We're going to see how many countries you all can name on each continent. And while you're walking around, learn the names of your classmates and at least one thing they like to do. This will be our home base for the next year, so get to know one another."

It took a moment before anyone stood up, but soon we were all walking around, writing on the maps and meeting each other. The room got loud with talking and laughter. It felt totally different and completely normal at the same time.

I didn't see Adeline again until after lunch, in algebra class. Our teacher wore a tie that was covered in numbers with goofy faces. He had written his name—Mr. Djondo—on the board and explained, "It's pronounced *Jondo*. The *D* is silent."

When he took attendance, Mr. Djondo paused at my name. "Is it Ma-*ken*-na, or Ma-*kay*-na?"

"Ma-*kay*-na," I answered, surprised that he had asked. Teachers usually mispronounced my name and I had to correct them. "Thanks for checking," I added.

He nodded. "Names matter. And so do numbers! Let's get started."

When the final bell rang that afternoon, I ran out of the building to get to the Metro. On the train ride, I scrolled through my Instagram feed, looking at all the first-day-back outfits everyone had posted. Someone named Evette P sent a photo of her super-cool platform shoes. I clicked *like*, and imagined what outfit I would wear with those shoes.

When I got to my old school, I went straight to the big

tree on the front lawn. Before she and Grandad moved, Gran used to pick up Amari and me every afternoon, and this is where she waited. Today, when Amari came outside, the first place she looked was under that tree. She smiled when she saw me and raced over. "Makena!" she said breathlessly. "It was awesome to be back in person. I have so much to tell you!"

I grinned. "Me, too."

As soon as we got home, I started to call Mom. My phone buzzed before I could dial.

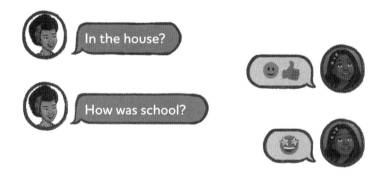

Before I started my homework, I went up to my room and opened my art journal. My brain was buzzing from the day and all the details I wanted to remember, so I spent a few minutes sketching. Drawing always calms me and helps me focus. I doodled some of the hairstyles, faces, and clothes I'd seen that day. Pretty soon I was planning my outfit for tomorrow, looking forward to another new day.

WE WALK TOGETHER

Chapter 4

After school the next day, I met Amari at the tree. Uncle Alex was there, too. He was taking us to volunteer at the food pantry that was part of the new community center. Uncle Alex had been helping out there for several weeks, but it was the first time Amari and I were going.

"You girls are gonna love this place," he said as he drove us the short distance to Riverfront Community Center. "It's big and bright, and there's plenty of space for the food pantry."

"I can't wait to see it," I said.

Riverfront Community Center was tucked at the edge of Anacostia Park by one of the curves in the river. Uncle Alex parked and we walked inside. I stopped short in the main entrance. There was an enormous mural of the park, created with more colors than I could name. It was filled with people of all ages and races, walking, riding bikes, climbing on playground equipment, sitting on benches, and having picnics in the grass. There were dancers and musicians, tennis and soccer players, roller skaters, and runners. At the bottom of the painting were the hand-lettered words "We Walk Together." It was spectacular.

"Come on, Makena! You always get swallowed up by art!" Amari dragged me along.

"The food pantry was the first part of the center to open," Uncle Alex said as we followed him down a hallway. "The center's going to roll out all types of classes and performances here in the next few weeks, and there will be rotating art exhibits." Uncle Alex pushed open a set of glass doors. "Here we are."

"Well, Alex Cook! I wasn't sure you'd make it," a tiny, bright-eyed woman said when we came in. She wore baggy jeans, a faded T-shirt, and a brightly colored head wrap. I liked her right away.

"Dahlia!" Uncle Alex shook her hand. "Sorry we're running late. These are my nieces, Makena and Amari Williams. How much do you still have for them to do?"

Dahlia winked at us. "Enough! Don't worry! Can you take care of the delivery in back?"

Uncle Alex left and Dahlia walked Amari and me across the room. There were a couple of teenagers and another man and woman already working at a row of prep tables set up in front of shelves stocked with boxes and cans of food. "Each table has a list of items that go into each box."

I saw what the others were doing and said, "So, our job

is finding the food on the shelves and packing it?"

"Yes, please. These boxes will be delivered to senior citizens and others who aren't able to come to the center."

"Our Uncle Alex helps with deliveries," Amari said proudly.

Dahlia smiled. "He's one of our best volunteers. I'm grateful for his help—and yours."

Amari and I got busy. It was easy to get into the rhythm of work, chatting with Dahlia and the others. Working at the food pantry reminded me of how much I missed the sights, sounds, and people at the restaurant. I thought about Grandad's saying, *Food brings people together.* Helping here was another way to feed people and feel connected.

We'd just packed the last box when Uncle Alex came back. "Our work here is done, and we've got some time before I need to get you girls home. Want to check out—"

"The gym? Yes!" Amari said. "I'll show you how to shoot hoops, Uncle Alex."

Uncle Alex rolled his eyes.

"Right. That's real funny. You in, Kay?"

"I want to look at the art. I'll catch up with you guys in a little while."

Dahlia told me where to find the exhibit space. It was a room with high ceilings and wide windows that faced the Anacostia River. A sign by the door said, "Community Creations: Knitting the Past into the Present." Displayed right next to the sign was a beautiful bulky pullover in a deep burgundy color. The front was covered with hands of different sizes, knitted in different shades of brown, all holding up this incredible golden sun. All around the gallery were jackets and dresses and capes knitted with pictures or messages or boldly colored three-dimensional designs. Was it art, or was it fashion? I thought of Auntie Bling, who would love everything here, and of Gran, who could probably *make* everything here.

"Wow," I breathed. I couldn't take my eyes off the display.

"I know, right?" a voice beside me agreed.

I turned to see a girl with long curly hair. My eyes went wide when I saw her platform shoes.

"I recognize those shoes," I said. "Are you Evette P?"

The girl looked as surprised as I felt. "I am. Makena? Whoa, I can't believe it's really you, in real life," she blushed.

"Those shoes are great," I said. "Where did you get them?"

Evette smiled. "My grandma's closet."

"Great find! Are they comfortable?"

"Surprisingly, yes," she said. "This is my friend Maritza," she said, waving to a girl in a soccer uniform who was looking at a knit scarf.

Maritza joined us. "I wouldn't last five minutes in those," she gestured to the platforms. "I'm more of a sneaker girl."

"Well, the ones you're wearing are cool," I said, admiring the teal stripe. "I've never seen that design before. Can I take a picture?" I pulled out my phone.

Now Maritza looked surprised. "Sure. Wow. I didn't wake up today thinking someone would want a picture of my soccer style."

"Why not?" I said, clicking a few shots. "Everyone's clothes make a statement. It's about how you feel or who you are. And you're active."

I motioned for Evette to stand next to Maritza so I could take a picture of both of them. "And Evette's statement is about mixing things from the past with things from today." I lowered my phone. "Right?"

"Yes!" Evette agreed eagerly. "I like to take something that doesn't fit right, or that I don't wear anymore, and turn it into something else that I like better. Like turn a dress into a top, or old pants into a bag. You know—upcycling."

"Have you ever been to Cherry Blossoms?" I asked. Both

girls shook their heads. "It's the best, and it's not too far from here."

"Maybe we could go sometime," Evette said. "Together."

"I'm in!" said Maritza. "That sounds fun."

"Totally!" I said. We exchanged numbers, which is when I saw the time on my phone. "I gotta go," I said as I dashed to the door. "See ya!"

"Bye," Maritza and Evette called.

On my way to the gym, I passed the big mural again. *We Walk Together.* I smiled, knowing that I had just met two new friends to walk with.

A POWERFUL THING

Chapter 5

By Wednesday I'd met a bunch of kids from my remote classes. A lot of them had been commenting on my posts all summer, and it was fun to finally talk to them in person. My favorite class, besides art, was going to be social studies. Maybe it was because of the activity we'd done on the first day, but everyone seemed to get along. I really liked talking to Adeline, and when Ms. Jacobs-Lee announced a group project, Adeline and I agreed to work together.

Adeline and I met for lunch that day and then headed to algebra together. The person at Mr. Djondo's desk was *not* Mr. Djondo. It was a substitute who hurriedly told us her name was Ms. Allyn. She rushed through attendance, barely looking at us, and pronounced my name "Macky-na." I wanted to correct her, but she jumped right into the lesson.

"Where do you suppose Mr. Djondo is?" I whispered to Adeline.

Ms. Allyn's arm stopped in front of the whiteboard. "Adeline, do you have a question?"

I squirmed in my seat. "Um, I'm Makena."

"Let's just focus on the board, Adeline," she said, like she hadn't heard me.

I glanced around. Adeline and I were the only two brown-skinned girls in the class—and we weren't even the same brown. I raised my hand.

"Excuse me—" I tilted my head toward Adeline's desk. "That's Adeline. I'm Makena."

"Stop disrupting class, please!" Ms. Allyn said sharply. She turned her back. "Now, all eyes on the board."

Adeline raised her eyebrows at me and looked down at her textbook.

I was stunned. I wasn't used to getting scolded at school, and no teacher had ever cared so little about getting names— or students—right. I tried to pay attention, but I was distracted.

After class, Adeline and I walked out of the room together. She spoke before I could.

"I don't know what happened in there," she said. "Do you think we look alike?" she asked.

We were passing a display case in the hall. I stared at our reflections. "Not even close," I said.

"I don't think so either," Adeline said, clearly as annoyed as I was. "See you tomorrow, Ma-KAY-na," she said loudly.

Najee and I took the train home together, and I told him about the name thing. He was quiet for a while, and then he said, "My dad used to say a name is a powerful thing. I'm named after him."

I bit my lip. Najee's father was a soldier who'd been killed fighting in Iraq.

"All I know, Makena, is that your name is something it's totally okay to stand up for." He gave me a half smile. "That's coming from someone who's always saying, 'I'm Nah-*jay*, not Nah-*jee*.'"

"You're right," I said thinking about when Mr. Djondo took the time to learn my name. "My real algebra teacher says names matter."

Najee nodded. "True that."

When Amari and I got home, I sprawled across my bed. I couldn't stop thinking about the mix-up, or what Najee had said.

I have four names: Makena means "happy one" in Swahili; Lilias was my dad's mom, who died when he was a boy; Cook, for Mom's family, and Williams. They all matter, and they make me who I am. Why couldn't that substitute teacher see that Adeline and I were two different girls? I sat up suddenly, staring at the jumble of shoes on the floor of my closet. I got an idea.

I pulled out one black flat with a bow on the toe, and one shiny black loafer in fake croc. Two different shoes. I dug my phone out and took a picture of the shoes. I posted it with the caption, "Just because we're both black doesn't mean we're the same."

I took out my pile of books and started on homework. In seconds, there were pings. I counted ten before I looked.

"What is going on?" Amari came in, curious. I grabbed my phone before she could, and scrolled, reading the comments out loud.

makenashine Just because we're both black doesn't mean we're the same.

itza.soccerchica: each one is unique

bianca_b: What?

blingbling: Totally different soles 👞

naj: I'm a guy, and even I know these are not the same.

earthyevette: Be proud of being different.

madison0213: Cute

adeline_: not even close 💚💚

☆ ♡ ☺

"I don't get it," Amari said. "Why'd you post mismatched shoes?"

"It was a sort of experiment," I said. "Some people *didn't* get it, but I'm glad that so many did!"

The next day was Friday, and Amari had basketball practice after school. I got permission to meet Evette and Maritza at Cherry Blossoms. Evie and I dove into the racks right away and found a bunch of cute stuff. Itza wandered around for bit but didn't pick up a single thing. "Don't you want to try anything on?" I asked.

"I do," Itza nodded, but she looked discouraged. "I'm just not much of a shopper. I never know where to start."

"I can help you find something that's your style if you want," I said. "Did you see that bright blue shirt with the lightning bolt by the door? It would look good with these," I said, pulling a pair of leggings off a shelf.

Itza's eyes brightened. "Oh, yeah! Cool. Thanks."

"And maybe this?" Evie said, handing Itza a denim jacket. She grinned at me. "You can't go wrong with a denim jacket."

We bustled Itza into a fitting room. A few minutes later, she opened the curtain tentatively. "What do you think?"

I tilted my head. "That blue is beautiful on you. But let's try different pants. And cuff the jacket," I called as I went in search of some skinny jeans. In a moment, I was back. "This would look good with brown ankle boots," I said, tossing the pants to Itza over the curtain.

"Boots?" Itza repeated, sounding doubtful.

"My grandma might have some in her closet," Evie said. "I'll check."

When Itza opened the curtain again, she was grinning. "I *love* it," she said. "Makena, you're so good at this."

"Aw, thanks," I smiled. "You still look sporty ... but we kicked it up a notch. Let me take a picture."

"You *are* good at this," Evie said. "You could start your own YouTube channel to show people how to put outfits together."

"Yeah, right," I said. "Who'd watch that?"

"We would!" Evie and Itza said at the same time.

I shook my head. "Well, there's zero chance my mom and dad would let me start my own channel."

"You still have really good ideas," Evie said.

Itza nodded as she headed back into the dressing room. "Would you send me that picture?" she asked. "I can't buy all this stuff today, but I want to remember what it looks like."

WHEN RIGHT GOES WRONG

Chapter 6

The weather was perfect on the day of the food truck festival. It was sunny, and the air was brisk but not cold. Mom, Dad, Amari, and I decided to bike to Anacostia Park. I wore jeans and my "Black Girls Rule" sweatshirt. For a pop of color, I added a crocheted scarf that Gran had made me in metallic yarns.

WHEN RIGHT GOES WRONG

We took a longer route through Anacostia so we could
pass Cedar Hill, the big house that sits up on W Street.
It's where the Black abolitionist Frederick Douglass lived
over a hundred years ago. He was born into slavery, but
he escaped and became a speaker and activist at the time
of the Civil War. Our family had taken the guided tour of
the house before the pandemic. On the tour I'd learned that
Frederick Douglass was the most photographed American
of his time—even more than President Abraham Lincoln.
I saw photos of Frederick Douglass decked out, wearing
suits with crisp white shirts and fancy ties. Mom says he
was always dressed well because he wanted to show people

what a free, dignified Black man looked like. I think about that every time we pass his house.

I took the lead as we turned on MLK Avenue, past the Big Chair. There used to be a furniture company on that corner. The store is gone, but the chair is still there, looking like something from a giant's dining room. The Martin Luther King Jr. Day parade marches past the chair every year. Dad says it's a landmark in Anacostia, just like the Washington Monument is a landmark in Capitol Hill.

"Careful, now!" Dad called out as we navigated through a traffic light. When we got to the community center, we locked our bikes to the bright red racks along the path.

The park was already crowded as we made our way to the food trucks. In addition to the festival, there was a soccer game and a flea market, and a band was setting up to play. Cruisin' Cook was one of two dozen food vendors parked near the entrance to the community center. The gold and white canopy on Uncle Alex's truck was flapping over the window, and people were already milling around. Jazz music played out of his speakers, and the delicious smells of his beef and cheddar hand pies and his mumbo sauce made my mouth water. Uncle Alex leaned out the window and waved.

"He's getting a good-size crowd," Dad said, as we stood back watching.

The line of customers continued to grow. I saw some neighbors from our block, including Jerome and Stella. There were even some kids and families from my old elementary school.

"Let's go check out the flea market and come back later," Mom said.

"I'm meeting Najee here," I said. "Can I wait?"

"Okay," Mom said. "But stay around here, close to Uncle Alex's truck."

In a few minutes, Najee wandered up the path. He was wearing ripped jeans, a neon green hoodie, and sneakers.

I smiled. "You brought lots of attitude today, huh?"

"I brought a lot of appetite!" He grinned. "Can't we cut the line?"

I laughed. "Are you kidding? Uncle Alex would just put us to work."

"Well, the line's pretty long," Najee said. "Let's check out the music."

On our way across the grass, I stopped. "Look at that little kid over there. She's all by herself.

"Where?" Najee turned.

A little red-headed girl was standing on the path. She couldn't have been more than three years old. I frowned. "The playground's close by. Maybe she wandered off."

Najee and I walked toward her, and I scanned the

grown-ups gathered around the swings. No one seemed to be looking for a child. As we got closer, I could see that her face was flushed, and her round cheeks were wet from crying. I thought about a time Amari got separated from me and Mom when we were at the grocery store. I found her in the cereal aisle, still as a statue, her face covered in tears. She'd been too scared to move or make a sound.

"Hey there," Najee said, kneeling down. "Are you lost, baby girl?"

The little girl blinked at us, wide-eyed, and nodded.

"Were you at the playground?" I asked, pointing to the swings. She stared at me without answering.

"What's your name?" Najee asked.

"Wexi," the little girl answered.

"Lexi?" Najee translated. She wagged her head.

"We'll help you find your mommy, Lexi," I told her. "Don't be scared. We'll walk with you. You want to hold my hand?"

She sat down right on the concrete.

"That's okay." Najee scooped her up. "I've got a cousin just about your age," he told her. She sniffed and stopped crying. We wound our way slowly around the playground, waiting for Lexi to recognize someone, or for someone to recognize her.

I scanned the crowds, thinking I might have to stand up on a bench and start yelling for everyone's attention, when Lexi laughed. I turned to see that Najee had put up his hood. He was pulling it down over his eyes and then back up again, saying "PEEK!" to Lexi. But after a moment, Lexi started whimpering. "I want my mommy."

"What are you two *doing* to that child?" a voice boomed.

I turned around to see a gray-haired White woman, red-faced and out of breath.

"Do you know this girl?" Najee asked, turning so that Lexi was facing the woman.

Lexi whimpered again.

The woman took a step back, clutching her purse tight against her side. She looked Najee up and down. "Where are you taking her?" she demanded.

"Um, wait—we're—" I started to explain.

But the woman didn't pay any attention to me. She stared at Najee and said, "I saw you. You're hurting her."

"That's not true," I said. "We're trying to help her."

The woman glanced at me. She looked me over, reading the words on my sweatshirt. "Oh, please," she muttered, turning back to Najee. "Give me this child."

Just then, a uniformed park ranger on a scooter rolled up. "Is there a problem here?" she asked in a crisp voice.

The White woman hesitated. Then she said with a straight face, "That boy in the hoodie was dragging this child somewhere." She glanced at me. "This one was with him."

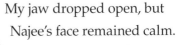

My jaw dropped open, but Najee's face remained calm. *What universe is this woman from?* I wondered.

The ranger looked from me to Najee to Lexi. "Are you related to the girl?" she asked the woman.

"Well, I—I—" the woman sputtered.

"Lexi is lost and we're trying to find her parents," Najee said to the ranger.

"Okaaay." The ranger gave him a long look. "Can you—"

"Lexi!" a voice shouted. "Oh my gosh!" A woman with hair the same red as Lexi's came running at full speed.

"Mama!" Lexi cried.

The woman with red hair scooped Lexi into her arms. "Are you okay, sweetie?"

For a moment, I froze. Who would Lexi's mother

believe? Najee and me or the woman?

Lexi smiled. "Peek," she said, pointing at Najee.

Najee grinned and pulled his hoodie over his eyes and then peeked at her. She giggled.

Lexi's mom hugged her tighter. "I turned my head for one second, and she was just gone!"

"It seems these kids found her and tried to help," the ranger said.

"Thank you," Lexi's mom said. "Both of you." She shook Najee's hand and then mine.

"I think we're done here," the ranger said to the woman who'd caused the scene. The woman glared at Najee and then left without saying another word.

Lexi's mom thanked us again. "Bye, Lexi," I called as Najee waved. Neither of us said anything for a moment. "What was that?" I asked finally.

"It's livin' while being Black," Najee said.

The two girls from that day at Cherry Blossoms with Amari flickered in my mind. *That woman saw just what she wanted to see*, I thought. *Not what was!*

WORDS HURT
Chapter 7

Najee decided he wasn't hungry and left the festival. I headed back to Uncle Alex's food truck. There was still a line, but since I wasn't feeling that hungry myself, I sat down on a bench. It wasn't long before my family showed up.

"Where's Najee?" Dad asked, looking around.

"What happened?" Mom said, looking at my face.

I glanced away. "Nothing."

"Makena?" Mom used her tell-the-truth tone. So I told them about Lexi and the out-of-control woman.

"That's totally racist," Amari said, sitting down next to me.

"She wouldn't listen to either of us," I said.

Mom sat down on my other side and put her arm around my shoulder. "Did you feel afraid?" Mom asked.

I shook my head. "It was more like…confused. At first I couldn't believe somebody would just make up a story about someone she didn't even know. How could she do that? Then, the ugly way she called Najee *that boy*…"

"She said it like that?" Dad asked.

"Yes," I said, thinking of what Najee had said about

46

names. "Like he wasn't even a real person with a real name and a real life! She claimed that he was trying to hurt Lexi."

Amari gasped. "Najee would never hurt anyone."

"Of course he wouldn't," Dad said.

"And when *I* tried to explain things, she froze me out. Like Black girls don't count as people at all." I remembered how the woman had looked me up and down. "She made me feel invisible and terrible at the same time."

"Listen," Dad said. "You aren't either of those things. Unfortunately, we know that people don't always treat us fairly. But you can't be afraid to do what you know is right."

Mom nodded. "You're a strong girl who helped a lost child. You and Najee made the right choice. I'm proud of the way you handled yourself."

As I leaned into Mom's hug, I couldn't help but think that my actions hadn't changed how that woman saw—or thought about—Black people. Was there anything that would?

I had plans to meet Evie and Itza at Riverfront the next day. They were both in the lounge when I got there, and Evie was showing Itza how she'd made her tote bag out of an old T-shirt.

"That's a cool idea," I said, plopping down at the table.

"You could post this, right?" Itza asked.

When I didn't pull out my phone right away, Evie peered at me. "Are you okay?"

I shook my head and told them what had happened at the park.

"She was like some ridiculous meme, screaming at us," I said, describing the White woman.

"That could happen to my brother in a few years," Evie said. "Bud has brown skin—darker than mine..." her voice trailed off. "He wouldn't hurt a worm, let alone a kid. But just because he's Black, some people might think..." She didn't finish her thought.

"That's absurd," Itza said.

"It's discrimination," I said.

"It can happen in families, too," Evie said quietly.

I looked at her. "What do you mean?"

"My mom's side of our family is Black, and my dad's side is White," she said. "For as long as I can remember, the two sides have always been separate. Birthdays. Holidays." Evie paused. "I recently found out that my Grandma Peeters said some horrible things to my Gran E years ago. Grandma made assumptions about Gran E without any facts, just because she's Black."

"That's so sad," Itza whispered.

"Wow. That's really tough," I shook my head. "I wish I knew what to do to make people look at us, see us for who we are, without judging or making assumptions. But how can we *do* that?"

Evie looked thoughtful. "You did that with the post about the two black shoes," she said.

"Did I?" I asked.

"Yes!" Itza said. "You made the point that there's more to a person than the color of her skin. That post totally made people think."

"You're good at making a statement with fashion, Makena," Evie said.

"Well, I was wearing a "Black Girls Rule" sweatshirt yesterday, and that woman looked at the words—and at me—as if they didn't matter."

"But *you* know they do," Itza said. "I bet someone saw those words and felt stronger because of you."

"Maybe," I said, wondering if Itza was right.

FASHION SPEAKS
Chapter 8

The next day I dressed in black jeans and a T-shirt I'd gotten at an anti-racism march. It was black, with large white letters on it.

"JUSTICE."

I decided to let this outfit speak for itself. I took a selfie and posted it without a caption.

"Aw, look at that shirt!" Najee said to me on the Metro.

"Yeah, I've been thinking a lot about this word," I said. "And I'm really, really sorry about Saturday!"

He rolled his eyes. "What? *You* weren't the one who was out of order," he said. Then he shrugged. "And I was not trying to get into a beef with that woman." As we got off the train and walked to school, Najee said, "The only important thing was finding Lexi's mother. Anybody could have snatched her."

I hesitated and then said, "I think that's what the woman was accusing *us* of doing."

Najee didn't miss a beat. "She was," he said, taking the steps two at a time. "It was hard not to tell her my opinion about her opinion, but I had to focus on the task at hand."

"I don't know how you did that." I thought about how calm Najee had been at the park. The way that White woman spat out her words had made my insides wrinkle. I know I looked shocked when she'd told the ranger that Najee had been *dragging* Lexi through the park. But I remember Najee's face staying still. "How did you stay so calm?"

"I saw my dad do that a few times," Najee said solemnly. "He always told me, 'Don't yell back. Make your words matter, not how loud you're talking.'"

Najee threw me the peace sign and melted into the hallway.

When Adeline and I met in the cafeteria at lunch, I checked my phone. I was shocked!

"My morning post got over two hundred likes!" I told her as I scrolled. Gran had responded with, "Justice is always in style," and a wink emoji. Auntie Bling sent me a link with the message, "Check out Carlotta Walls."

"Who's Carlotta Walls?" I wondered out loud.

"Some clothing designer?" Adeline asked, smothering her fish sticks with ketchup.

I clicked on the link. "Oh! She was one of the Little Rock

Nine," I said, munching and reading. "They were the first Black kids to go to an all-White high school in Little Rock, Arkansas, in 1957."

"I've heard about them," Adeline said. "Didn't the National Guard block the entrance to the building, because White people didn't want them in the school?"

I nodded. "President Eisenhower had to send in more troops to escort them inside. This article says Carlotta was determined to go because the school had much better books and resources than the Black schools. It was such a big deal that the dress she wore is in the National Museum of African American History and Culture. Look!"

Adeline scooted over to squint at my screen.

There was a photo of the dress Carlotta had worn on her first day of school. It was black with blue and white geometric shapes and letters of the alphabet in pops of teal. "Carlotta's mom usually made all her clothes," I read to Adeline. "She was an excellent seamstress, but this dress had come from a store. Carlotta's great-uncle had given them the money to buy it because he wanted her to have something special for such an important occasion."

I paused, thinking of the outfit I'd chosen for my first day of seventh grade. I'd wanted to make a statement. I wondered if Carlotta had wanted to do the same thing. "Maybe she chose that dress with the alphabet print as a way of telling her teachers and classmates that she was determined to learn," I said to Adeline.

"Yeah," Adeline said slowly. "Maybe."

There was another photo, of Carlotta and the other eight kids standing beside a line of soldiers in uniform.

"That must have been really hard for those kids to do," Adeline murmured.

I looked closely at the picture of the soldiers with their guns. "And scary, too."

After dinner that night, I texted Auntie Bling to thank her for clueing me in to Carlotta Walls. She got right back to me.

Keep up your combo of fashion and feeling! Look up Harlem's Fashion Row, too. See how other cool Black women are finding their purpose in fashion.

I opened my laptop and typed "Harlem's Fashion Row" in the search bar. I found the website and started clicking through images on Instagram. The clothes—and the people designing them—were so cool.

A while later, Mom popped her head in my room.

"Mom, check this out," I said, showing her my screen. "Did you know that less than five percent of the designers at most fashion houses are people of color?"

"I did not," Mom said. She nodded toward my stack of unopened books. "It looks like you've done less than five percent of your homework."

I looked at the time. "Oops. Auntie Bling sent me some interesting stuff."

Mom read Auntie Bling's text. "Your aunt's friend Brandice started Harlem's Fashion Row," Mom said, handing me my phone. "She wants designers of color to have the same opportunites as other designers."

"Kind of like how Carlotta Walls wanted to have the

same opportunities as the White kids in her town." I told Mom about the other link Auntie Bling had sent me. Of course Mom knew about the Little Rock Nine, but she didn't know Carlotta's dress was in a museum.

"Fashion can be a form of activism," Mom said. "And I wouldn't be surprised if one day that was your purpose. But right now," Mom handed me my algebra book, "math is your purpose."

I closed my laptop and smiled at Mom. "I'm on it."

On Sunday I spent a few hours at Riverfront, helping at the food pantry. Afterward, I met Evie and Itza in the lounge. When Itza saw the butterfly on my shirt, she smiled. "Every time I see butterflies, I think of you, Makena."

"Did you guys know monarch butterflies are endangered?" Evie asked, sitting down at the art table. "We need to take better care of nature."

Evie had organized a cleanup project for a spot along the Anacostia River. "You're making a good start by taking care of the river," I pointed out. I picked up a purple marker and started sketching a butterfly.

"True, but I wish there was more we could do," Evie said. "I mean, it's going to be our world someday."

"Well, we don't need to wait until we grow up to make a difference," said Itza as she started doodling. "We can start now, making the kind of world we want to live in."

I put my marker down. "I want to live in a world where who you are inside matters more than what you look like outside." I thought about Carlotta Walls and the eight other Black kids, standing next to armed soldiers, trying to get into school.

"I want a world where a community can be full of people of different backgrounds and beliefs, but still be united," Itza said.

Evie turned to me with excitement. "We should put our ideas online, like you do with your fashion posts. We'll share what we're doing to fight pollution, and racism, and other issues we care about."

"It could be a place for other kids to share what they're doing, too," Itza said. "Makena, could you show us how to start a page?"

"Sure," I said. "If my parents say it's okay. What should we call it?"

Evie picked up a purple marker and a piece of poster board. In elegant script, she wrote, "World by Us." She said, "That's what we'll call it—and that's what we'll *make* it."

"Yes," I said, adding a butterfly in one corner. "A world by us will be beautiful."

ONE COLD DAY
Chapter 9

I had been so good at remembering my house key every day that Amari had become really lazy about bringing hers. It always worked out, since the only times we didn't come home together was when Dad or Mom or Uncle Alex picked her up from school. But on a cold Friday in October, I couldn't find *my* key.

"What's taking so long?" Amari asked. She was rubbing her hands together because she'd forgotten her gloves.

I pulled everything out of my backpack. No key. "You don't have yours?"

She gave me an exasperated sigh. "I told you I lost it!"

"Again? Get the spare from under the porch rail."

Amari stomped across the porch. "It's not here either!" She looked at me sheepishly. "I—I might have used it the last time I lost my key."

"So now the spare is lost?"

"Uh-huh."

"Amari!"

"Sorry!" Amari cried. "What now?"

I thought about calling Uncle Alex—he had a key. But

the food truck wasn't like a restaurant. He was by himself, so he couldn't just leave.

"Well, I'm cold!" Amari said. I didn't admit it, but I was, too.

"Okay. Let's try a window. I'll try the kitchen, and you go around the side to try the dining room."

We separated. I dragged the patio bench under the high kitchen window and climbed on it. Then I stood up to reach the window. It was locked.

"The ones in the dining room are locked!" Amari called. "I could break a basement window …"

"Don't you dare!" I shouted. "Try that window by the fireplace on the other side. Didn't Dad have it open last week?"

"I think so!" she yelled.

I hopped off the bench and headed back to the front porch. A dog began to bark close by.

Sirens were blaring somewhere in the neighborhood. *Probably an ambulance*, I thought. The sounds got closer and closer.

"There's no way in," Amari said, joining me on the porch. "I'm gonna have to call Mom." She took off her backpack and began searching for her phone.

All at once, red and blue lights were flashing in front of our house, and doors were slamming on a police car. Two officers, one Black and one White, were suddenly at the bottom of the porch steps.

"I need you both to put your hands where I can see them," the Black officer said sternly.

My heart began pounding. I tried to think of what our parents had taught us to do in a moment like this. I could only hear my Dad's words:

Remember your sister.
I lifted my arms very slowly, darting my eyes at Amari. She was still holding her backpack, frozen-scared, just like she'd been all those years ago in the

grocery store. Just like Lexi had been in the park.

"Drop the bag and put your hands up!" the White officer demanded. I was scared. What would happen if Amari didn't move fast enough?

"Amari," I whispered, trying to keep my voice steady. "Do what they say."

That dog was going crazy now.

"We got a report of two Black women breaking into a house on U Street," the White officer said.

The Black officer stepped closer, and I felt my knees shaking. "But you two are just kids…" he said, looking around as if he expected someone else.

Suddenly I heard our neighbor Jerome shouting, "Makena? Amari? Are you okay? Did someone try to break in?" I saw him running toward our house, his dreadlocks flying.

Stella was right behind him. "Hey! These girls are our neighbors!" she said loudly. "What's going on?"

"This is *your* house?" the Black officer asked me.

"Yes," I said, finally finding my voice. He took a step back, and Amari started to cry.

"We—we were locked out," I hiccupped.

"There must be some kind of mistake here," the Black officer said.

Jerome came up to the porch and said to Amari and me, "Go to our house. I'll sort this out, and Stella will call your parents."

I was shaking so much that Stella took one of my hands, and one of Amari's. I had trouble walking down our steps. My feet wouldn't do what I wanted them to.

Across the street, in a house that had recently sold, a short, pale man I'd never seen before was standing at his gate with his arms crossed. Had he called the police on us? Our own neighbor?

Dad and Mom arrived together. Mom grabbed me and held me tight; then she knelt next to Amari, who was lying on a futon. She was awake, but she had been very still and very quiet. When she saw Mom, she started crying again.

"I lost the keys," she kept saying. "I lost the keys!"

"It's all right," Mom said, hugging her.

Dad put his hands on my shoulders and studied my face. I felt the sting of tears and closed my eyes. Dad wrapped his arms around me. "Let's go home."

My parents thanked Stella and Jerome. Back at our house, they took Amari and me up to their bedroom and settled us in their king-size bed. Mom went to make us some tea. Amari fell asleep right away. I couldn't.

The phones started buzzing. All the phones. Where was mine? I got up and walked unsteadily into my own room. Mom had placed my phone on the dresser, and it was buzzing its way to the edge. I looked at the text and picked it up. It was from Najee.

What did he even mean? I scrolled to our neighbor-hood news site. Somebody had posted a picture of us on the porch. I sat down hard on my bed. I didn't recognize either myself or my sister. I was watching two brown girls standing in front of a police officer with their hands up. We looked terrified, and from the angle of the picture, the officers looked huge.

I clicked my phone off.

Later on, the doorbell rang. I listened through my open door. I heard Mom, Dad, and Jerome. Turns out that the person who'd decided that we were breaking into our own house *was* the man across the street.

"So, he just called the police?" Dad got loud.

"The man said he didn't know who lived here," Jerome answered.

"Couldn't he see that they're children?" Mom asked.

I rolled over and pressed the pillow around my ears, but Mom's question was like a song I couldn't get out of my head. *Couldn't he see that they're children? Couldn't he see?*

No, Mom! I wanted to scream. That's the problem. He couldn't see that we're real people, with real names and lives and feelings. All he could see was that we're Black. I cried sad and mad tears, because none of it made any sense.

SEE ME, HEAR ME, KNOW ME

Chapter 10

I woke up in my own bed and squinted in the morning sun bouncing off my dresser mirror. Like light bouncing off a gold badge. Yesterday came back to me all of a sudden, making my head spin.

Yesterday Amari and I had been living our lives being regular girls. I'm Makena, the girl who loves drawing and clothes and making new friends. The lucky brown girl with a sister who isn't a pest and parents I can talk to and a family who loves food and feeding other people. And now, because one person didn't know or care who we were, all I could think about was the police staring at us on our own front porch. *Can I ever walk across it again without remembering those awful minutes?* I shivered.

Mom was always reminding me to focus on my breathing. In. Out. Slowly. One. Two. Three. Four. I closed my eyes and tried to concentrate on the breaths.

One.

The girls at the store who pretended Amari and I were invisible.

Two.

The teacher who couldn't be bothered to learn my name.

Three.

The woman in the park who didn't believe I was helping a little White girl.

Four.

A stranger across the street who assumed the worst because he didn't know me.

All of them had made up a new Makena who was invisible and who did bad things and had bad friends because that's what they figured all Black people did. It wasn't fair. *That* Makena didn't even exist. I opened my eyes. I had to figure out a way to get all those judgy people to understand. *To feel.* I reached for my journal and started drawing. But instead of pictures, words came out.

I'm so much more than what you see 👁

Don't guess—
ASK about
all the feels
inside me

That was it! I scrambled to my dresser and found a plain black T-shirt. Then I got my metallic fabric paints. I picked out a bright pink and carefully copied the last three lines. While the paint dried, I stared at the words. As I said them out loud over and over, I suddenly knew it wasn't enough this time for my clothes to make a statement.

Once the paint dried, I put the shirt on. I picked up my phone and started recording with the camera on a close-up of my face.

"My name is Makena Williams. Something happened to me, and I am not okay." My voice began to shake, but I kept talking. The words tumbled out.

"Yesterday, my sister and I forgot our house keys. Somebody across the street, who doesn't know us, called the police. The police came with sirens blaring and lights flashing. They didn't ask questions first. They ordered us to freeze with our hands up. On our own porch. They assumed we were two Black women trying to break in. I'm thirteen, and my sister is eleven. This is our *home*. Do you know what this feels like? It hurts."

I moved the camera to show my T-shirt.

"I am a person. *See* me for who I am. *Hear* what I say. Get to *know* me before you make up something about me. Judge me by my words and actions, not my race. See *me*. Hear *me*. Know *me*."

Wiping away the tear that I didn't mean to have, I stopped recording. I wasn't sure about posting it, but in a strange way I was glad I'd gotten my feelings out. I opened my bedroom door. Amari wasn't in her room, or in Mom and Dad's. I heard their voices in the kitchen and headed downstairs.

"Mom? Dad? Can I show you something?"

I sat with my arms folded, watching them watch the video. I got stomach jitters, because I had never shared so much of *me* before.

"Makena," Mom said, "this video is powerful."

"It's really brave," Amari said, nodding. "I could never do this. Just like I couldn't do anything on the porch." Her voice faded to a whisper as she looked at me. "I'm sorry—"

Dad lifted her chin. "Don't you ever apologize for someone else's mistake. The person who thought you and your sister were Black women breaking into a house was wrong. You were not. You hear me?"

Amari nodded again. "Are you going to post this?" she asked me.

I looked at Mom and Dad. "Can I?"

Dad looked concerned. "Are you sure you're ready to put yourself out there this way?"

I took a deep breath. I thought about what Mom had said weeks ago, about finding the courage to take action.

"I want people to know how it hurts to be judged by somebody who doesn't have all the facts! I want them to know what it feels like when they treat others—especially kids—like we don't have a voice, or like we don't even exist."

Mom glanced at Dad, who nodded. "We knew you would be determined when you were born two weeks early," she said.

"Can I post it then?"

"Yes, go ahead, Makena. Put your message out there for the world to see."

I typed, "See Me, Hear Me, Know Me," and hit *Share*.

A GIFT WORTH CELEBRATING

Chapter 11

After I posted the video, my social media was on fire. There were so many likes and comments that I could barely read them all.

I felt a rush of energy and hope. By that afternoon, some kids started making and sharing their own videos—my friends included. I was blown away by what they said.

Hello. My name is Adeline Joseph. Do you know what it's like when you're sitting somewhere, like the library, minding your own business, and you feel a stranger's fingers patting your head? My hair is a part of my body. I am not a pet that you pat. This style is called Bantu knots. If you are curious about it, you can ask me. But it is not okay to touch me. Hair is part of a person, you know.

A GIFT WORTH CELEBRATING

My name is Najee Warren Jr. I am the son of Janae Warren and Najee Warren Sr. Both of my parents served in the United States Army in Iraq. They fought to make this country safe. My mother came home. My father didn't. When you see me and treat me like a criminal without knowing anything about me, you disrespect my father, my mother, and me. I am a hero's son. In the video, Najee held up a case with a Purple Heart medal in it. See me.

I am Evette Peeters. My mother is Black, and my father is White. I love my family. I love who I am. People sometimes ask me if I'm Black or White. I am a girl. I am a human being. Why can't I just be me? I am part of all of my family. Get to know me for who I am.

Hi. My name is Maritza Ochoa. I am DC born and raised. I love school, fiestas, winning 5K races, and playing soccer. Like many people I know, I speak two languages. It drives me bananas when people assume we're not American just because we're speaking Spanish. I'm as American as you are. An American can speak one language or ten. Our differences make us stronger.

For a few minutes, I could only sit staring at my screen. No way could anybody watch these videos without feeling moved—and that was the whole point.

On Sunday afternoon, Amari and I were on the sofa rewatching the videos when the doorbell rang. As Dad answered it, Mom came in from the kitchen and headed for the door. "Come with me, girls. This visitor is here to see you two," she said.

Amari and I looked at each other. We got to the door at the same time. There, on our front porch, was the man from across the street. I stopped.

"Dad?" When I looked at my father's face, I realized that he and Mom weren't surprised by this visit. I was.

"Makena? Amari?" The man sounded nervous. "My name is Luke Brown. I'm the one who called the police two days ago."

"I know," I said, looking him in the eye.

"I'm here to apologize," he said.

I could feel Amari's shoulders tense next to me. Mom put her arm around her, and Dad came to stand behind me. I stepped out onto the porch, and Luke Brown stepped back.

"I didn't know this was your house," he said. "From where I stood, you looked like adults. I thought ... you were breaking in."

"Do you see us now?" I asked. "We're girls. We're your neighbors."

He looked from me to Amari. "I see that now. I'm really sorry."

I glanced at Dad as I pulled my phone from my pocket. "Can I show you something?" I asked Luke Brown.

He watched my video. He was quiet for a moment and then said, "You're right. I didn't see you for you. What I did was wrong. I'm going to work to be a better neighbor."

I didn't say anything, but I hoped that was true. He kind of nodded and turned away. Mom and Amari went inside. Dad and I watched him walk slowly back to his house.

"Are you okay?" Dad asked.

"It's so strange, Dad. Even though I wanted to hear him say that, the words don't quite make the hurt go away." After a moment, I said, "I'm glad I got to show him my video."

"Seems like what you're showing people is that if they just think a little harder, they wouldn't hurt each other in the first place," Dad said.

A few days later, I got a package in the mail from Auntie Bling. It was a black T-shirt with the words "See Me, Hear Me, Know Me" screen-printed in purple with a butterfly and a heart graphic. I ran my fingers across the letters. There was my idea, my first design, in real life. I was so proud. As I picked up the shirt to try it on, a note fluttered to the floor. I saw Auntie Bling's handwriting.

I read her note twice. Then I slipped the shirt on and studied it in the mirror. I'd always used fashion to express my feelings. With my video, I'd learned that sometimes it's important to speak up—and speak out—when you believe in something. Over the past week, it seemed that everyone at Aspire Academy was talking about the video posts. Kids

I didn't know were seeking me out because they had things to say but were too shy to say them online.

My eyes went back to Auntie Bling's word *power*. Maybe I *could* give other people the power to tell their own stories. What if kids could show and tell the world who they really are, how they really feel, in any style they chose? What if we had a show of fashion and art and spoken word, even music? Just like that, I had an idea.

POWERFUL STATEMENTS/
POWERFUL STYLE

Riverfront Community Center
Saturday, November 6 @ 6:00 pm

* Please bring a nonperishable food item to support
the Riverfront Community Center food pantry.

A GIFT WORTH CELEBRATING

With Uncle Alex's help, I found the right person to talk to at Riverfront Community Center about using one of the rooms to put on the show. I called it "Powerful Statements/ Powerful Style." My parents said I could announce it on my Instagram and on the World by Us website, too.

Gran and Grandad drove up from North Carolina for the showcase. They were with the rest of my family in the front row. Uncle Alex was doing a livestream so Auntie Bling could tune in from LA.

Just before the show started, I peeked out at the audience. The room was packed with kids from my school, and from Itza's and Evie's schools. Many of our Anacostia neighbors were there, too. Lots of different people. And we, a bunch of kids, had brought them together!

My stomach fluttered a little as I checked my phone. It was time.

The music started, which was my cue. I walked to center stage and stepped into the spotlight. I was wearing my "See Me, Hear Me, Know Me" tee with a long wrap skirt of colorful kente cloth. My butterfly hair clips glittered in the spotlight. When I reached the microphone, I spoke clearly.

"I'm Makena. I'm proud that my family's roots in Anacostia go back four generations. I came up with the words on my T-shirt because people weren't seeing the real me. They were only seeing that I was Black—if they saw me at all. I love West African kente cloth because the colors and patterns tell stories. The green in this skirt signifies renewal. I like wearing butterflies because they remind me that though change can be difficult, it can lead to something beautiful. With my fashion, I am always making a statement."

The audience clapped as I exited and Evie made her way across the stage. She was wearing platform shoes, a T-shirt that said "Earth Day Every Day," jeans, and a floppy felt hat.

"I am Evette," she said. "My mother's family is Black and my father's family is White. Today I wear platform shoes from one grandma, and this awesome hat from my other grandma." Evie flipped up the brim and smiled. "Just like fashion, my family mixes and matches!"

Itza came next wearing bike shorts, a pullover, a beanie, and sneakers. She was dribbling a soccer ball down the runway.

"I am Maritza and I'm always ready for action. I'm half Mexican, half Bolivian, and one hundred percent American soccer player."

One by one, others shared their stories and celebrated their style. One girl brought her keyboard and played a song she'd written called "The Equality March." A few kids showed their paintings. One boy had painted two trees whose multicolored branches had grown together without tangling. The painting was almost as tall as the artist.

When everyone had made their statements, we all gathered onstage for a bow. The audience was on its feet, clapping and cheering for us. All the other kids hopped off the stage and started mingling. I stood there, watching adults talking to kids and kids from different communities talking to each other. Seeing so many people come together was powerful.

Before I stepped off the stage, my phone rang. It was Auntie Bling. "Makena, I'm so proud!" she sounded as excited as I felt, and she didn't let me get a word in. "Do you know what you've just done? You've designed and directed a show! But the way you put fashion and feeling together, you've created something more. You've created a movement for justice!"

I shook my head. "I have? Wow. Thanks, Auntie Bling! Thanks for everything." I pressed the phone against my ear, trying to hear. It had gotten loud in the room. "I'll call you when there isn't so much noise."

"Go on," Auntie Bling said. "Enjoy the moment. I love you."

Her words were still swirling in my brain when I finally left the stage.

Ms. Jacobs-Lee was waiting to talk to me. "Makena, this was amazing! What inspired you to create this showcase with such an incredible message?" she asked.

We were standing in front of the big windows overlooking the Anacostia River. I saw the reflections of Itza, Evie, Adeline, and Najee in the background.

"Because I believe that when you take time to get to know people, you get to see who they truly are," I said.

I was so proud of what we'd done that I couldn't stop grinning. Just before I went to join my friends and family, I glimpsed my own reflection in the window.

It looked as if the river was flowing right through me. *Maybe it does*, I thought, *along with the strength of my ancestors, and the bravery of Black people before and the bravery of everyone in this room who works for change.*

Because of all those people, in that moment, I felt that Auntie Bling was right. I had created a movement for justice. And with the help of my friends, I was going to keep it going.

STANDING UP TO RACISM

Makena Williams is a fictional character, but her experiences are based on real racial injustices that many Black people face. Makena is treated unfairly because of the color of her skin. Maybe you've seen this happen to someone you know, or maybe you've been treated unfairly because of the color of your skin. Like Makena, you may want to be seen, heard, and known for who you are—not what you look like.

People make assumptions about others when they don't know much about an ethnicity, cultural background, or religious belief. How can we change false assumptions? By learning what we don't know.

Here are some ideas:

• With a parent or teacher, find five videos that help you learn about others' life experiences and points of view.

• Ask a librarian to help you look up articles about anti-racism or discover three books by authors of color whose main characters live differently than you.

• Learn another language, even if it means learning basic vocabulary or just a few phrases.

• Watch a show or movie featuring people from a different racial group than you.

• Research the racial makeup of your community to better under-stand the racial minorities in your city. Are there cultural events put on by that group you could attend?

• Find recipes to make food you've never tried before from a different ethnic group. Or seek out a new restaurant for your family's next night out.

To learn more about fighting racism, look for *A Smart Girl's Guide: Race & Inclusion.*

MEET BRANDICE DANIEL

Founder of Harlem's Fashion Row

Like Makena, I use clothes to send a message.

I grew up in Memphis, Tennessee. As a girl, I loved clothes and liked to redesign my shoes with rhinestones and a glue gun. My aunt was a model, and I loved hearing about her job and seeing the pictures of the beautiful clothes she got to wear. She encouraged my interest in clothes by giving me fashion magazines after she read them. My aunt saw something in me that I didn't yet see in myself.

I dreamed of working in fashion, but not necessarily as a model. I didn't know what other kind of work I could do until a teacher in college explained that there were many different kinds of jobs. After I graduated, I became a buyer for a clothing store. My job was to help decide what women's clothes the company would sell in stores all over the United States. I got to see so many different types of clothes and pick out the items I thought women would like most. I also met lots of interesting people.

My job was fun, but my big dream was to move to New York City, which is home to many famous fashion designers, department stores, and boutiques. I was scared to move to

A Harlem brownstone

such a big and busy city, but I didn't want to let fear stop me. I was 28 when I arrived in New York. I lived in Harlem, a neighborhood in Manhattan with tree-lined streets and beautiful brownstone buildings. Harlem is known as a center of Black culture, music, and art, and I loved being in a place with such a rich history. I also had fun exploring all the shops and restaurants in Harlem.

I got a job at an apparel company managing the way the clothes were made. I loved being part of the fashion industry, but I noticed something. Even though Black people spent millions of dollars on clothes every year, there were very few Black designers selling their fashions in major department stores. I thought someone should change that. At first, I didn't think it would be me. I didn't know many people in New York, and most

Hosting an event in 2013

influential people in the fashion industry didn't know me. But an idea was tugging at my heart. Designers of color needed to be seen, heard, and supported. After being in Harlem for a few years, I decided to produce a fashion show that would showcase the work of four Black designers.

Trying to achieve something big requires a team, so I had to ask for a lot of help. It wasn't always easy to convince people to say yes, but I didn't give up. On the night of the fashion show there was a line of people waiting to get in. The event turned out even better than I'd hoped, and I was so proud of the talented designers and their amazing work.

That fashion show was the start of my company. In 2007 I founded Harlem's Fashion Row to make sure designers of color have the same impact and connections as every other designer. Some people didn't think I was qualified to run this kind of company since I didn't have a lot of fashion friends or hadn't worked at a well-known fashion company. I didn't always think I was qualified either. There have been times when I've wanted to quit. That's when I think about the designers of the future. I know there are young kids who, like me and Makena, dream of working in the fashion industry. They need me to keep going today so Black people have opportunities tomorrow.

At a fashion exhibition in 2019

READER QUESTIONS

Use these questions to spark conversations about Makena's story.

1. Makena uses fashion to make statements. What other ways does she share her ideas and feelings? What do you think has the most impact?

2. When Makena is in social studies on her first day of school, she says, "It felt totally different and completely normal at the same time." What did she mean?

3. Makena experiences several forms of racism in the book. Which one impacted you the most? Why?

4. "They saw what they wanted to see," Makena tells her sister when the White girls cut in line at the clothing store. This kind of action is called a microaggression. It's a small act of excluding someone based on race. It may not seem like a big deal, but experiencing something like this over and over can make everyday encounters in life difficult or hurtful. How does Makena react to this microaggression? What does it say about her character?

5. Makena mentions two historic figures: Frederick Douglass and Carlotta Walls. What does Makena learn from the way they dressed?

6. Do you think Makena forgave her neighbor after he apologized? Why or why not? How would you react in that situation if you were Makena?

7. During the incident at the park, Najee follows his dad's advice: "Don't yell back. Make your words matter, not how loud you're talking." Is this good advice? Why or why not?

LOOK FOR BOOKS ABOUT
EVETTE AND MARITZA

Evette Peeters is a nature-lover full of crafty ideas for reusing and upcycling clothes. When she discovers a swimsuit in her grandmother's closet, she uncovers a secret from the past. Evette wants to know why her mother's side of the family, which is Black, and her father's side of the family, which is White, don't spend time together. Evette knows she can't change the past, but maybe she can change her family's future. One day Evette visits the river her grandmother used to swim in. The river is still beautiful, but it's polluted and needs help. Determined to heal the river, Evette organizes a cleanup day. Unexpectedly, the river shows her a way to heal the division her family. But will it work?

Maritza Ochoa is Bolivian on her mother's side, Mexican on her father's side, and 100 percent American soccer player. She dreams of playing for the US women's soccer team, and even coaching it someday. Her soccer teammate Violeta shares those dreams, too, but for her they are harder to reach. Violeta's family immigrated to the United States from El Salvador, and now her uncle may be sent back there, far away from his US family. Without the money he earns and the love and support he provides, the family is in distress. Maritza believes that families belong together. Can she find a way to help Violeta's family? With her friends Evette and Makena cheering her on, Maritza finds the courage to lead with her heart.

*Each sold separately. Find more books online at **americangirl.com**.*